To my Grandmother

VIKING
Published by the Penguin Group
Penguin Books USA, Inc., 375 Hudson Street, New York, New York 10014, U.S.A.
Penguin Books Ltd, 27 Wrights Lane, London W8 5TZ, England
Penguin Books Australia Ltd, Ringwood, Victoria, Australia
Penguin Books Canada Ltd, 10 Alcorn Avenue, Toronto, Ontario, Canada M4V 3B2
Penguin Books (N.Z.) Ltd, 182-190 Wairau Road, Auckland 10, New Zealand

Penguin Books Ltd, Registered Offices: Harmondsworth, Middlesex, England

First published in Great Britain by All Books for Children, 1997
First published in the United States of America by Viking,
a division of Penguin Books USA Inc., 1997

1 3 5 7 9 10 8 6 4 2

Library of Congress Catalog Card Number: 96-61352

ISBN 0-670-87473-6

Printed in Hong Kong

Rumble
in the
Jungle

Britta Teckentrup

Viking

The jungle was quiet and peaceful.
Lion was asleep, Crocodile was swaying with the ripples on the river, Giraffe was nibbling leaves, and Monkey was swinging between two vines.

Suddenly, there was a
tug on one of his vines, and
Monkey somersaulted into
the river with a splash!

"What was that?" he cried, looking up.
All he could see was four long legs.
It was Giraffe, munching on a vine.
Monkey's vine.

"Go back to your leaves!"
screeched Monkey. "Vines
are for swinging."
"There are lots of vines
in the jungle. Find another,"
answered Giraffe.

But Monkey was
pulling one end of the
vine. "I had it first!"
he shouted.

His friends and family
lined up to help him pull.
Giraffe slipped.

Crocodile came to her rescue, wrapping the vine around his strong tail. "No one can beat me," he boasted.

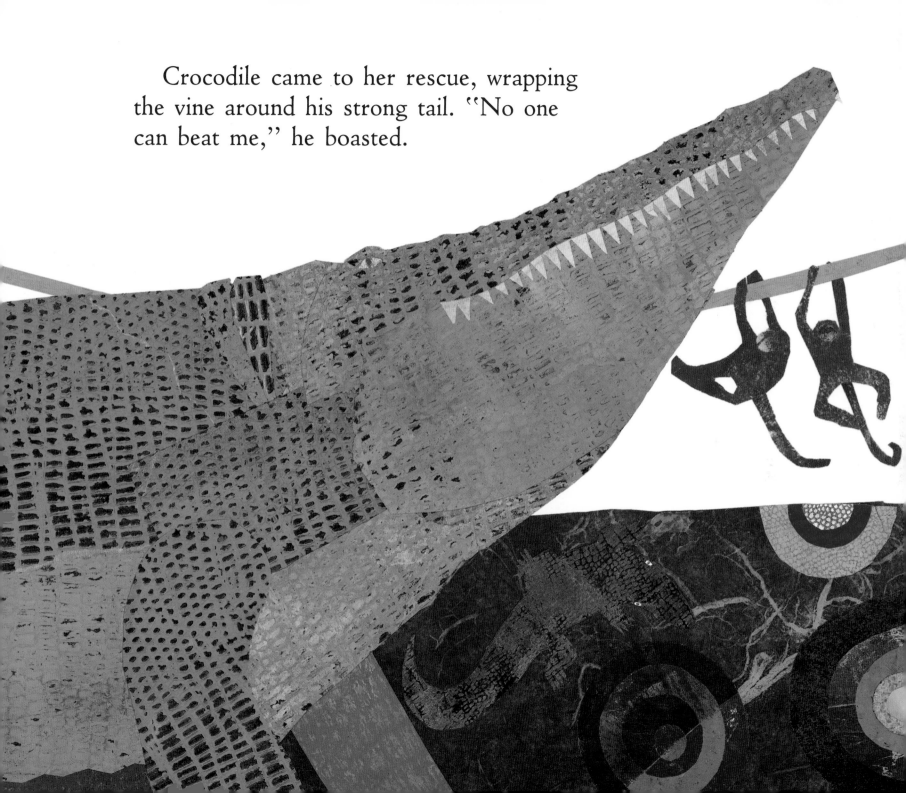

"I can," came a deep voice. And out
of the river climbed another Crocodile.
They glared at each other. "Let's see
who's stronger," they grumbled,
tugging at opposite ends.

Rhinoceros thumped up. "Oh, good, a fight!"
And he wrapped the end of Giraffe's vine
around his horn and began to pull.

Monkey's side started to slip. "This isn't fair," thought Elephant, who had been watching. Wrapping her trunk around the vine on Monkey's side, she heaved.

All day long,
the animals pulled and tugged.

First one side slipped a little . . .

. . . then the other side slipped a little.

Back . . .

        . . . and forth . . .

. . . they went.

By the end of the afternoon, Zebra, Tiger, and Warthog were tugging, too, and Parrot was cheering for both sides.

The sun went down and the moon rose up.
They were still tugging.
"I'll never give up," grunted Monkey.
"Oh yes you will!" gasped Giraffe.
And, at that moment . . .